Henry and Mudge
IN THE
Sparkle Days

The Fifth Book of Their Adventures

Story by Cynthia Rylant
Pictures by Suçie Stevenson

BRADBURY PRESS • NEW YORK

To Casey and Jane Rehm—CR

For Edwina—ss

THE HENRY AND MUDGE BOOKS

Text copyright © 1988 by Cynthia Rylant
Illustrations copyright © 1988 by Suçie Stevenson
All rights reserved. No part of this book may be reproduced or
transmitted in any form or by any means, electronic or
mechanical, including photocopying, recording, or by any
information storage and retrieval system, without permission in
writing from the Publisher.

Bradbury Press
An Affiliate of Macmillan, Inc.
866 Third Avenue, New York, N.Y. 10022
Collier Macmillan Canada, Inc.

Manufactured in the United States of America
10 9 8 7 6 5 4 3 2
The text of this book is set in 18 pt. Goudy Old Style.
The illustrations are pen-and-ink and watercolor, reproduced in full color.
Book design by Mina Greenstein.

Library of Congress Cataloging-in-Publication Data
Rylant, Cynthia.
Henry and Mudge in the sparkle days.
"The Henry and Mudge books"—Jacket.
Summary: In the winter Henry and his big dog Mudge
play in the snow, share a family Christmas Eve dinner,
and gather around a crackling winter fireplace.
[1. Winter—Fiction. 2. Dogs—Fiction]
I. Stevenson, Suçie, ill. II. Title. III. Title:
Henry and Mudge books.
PZ7.R982Hh 1988 [E] 86-26432
ISBN 0-02-778005-8

Contents

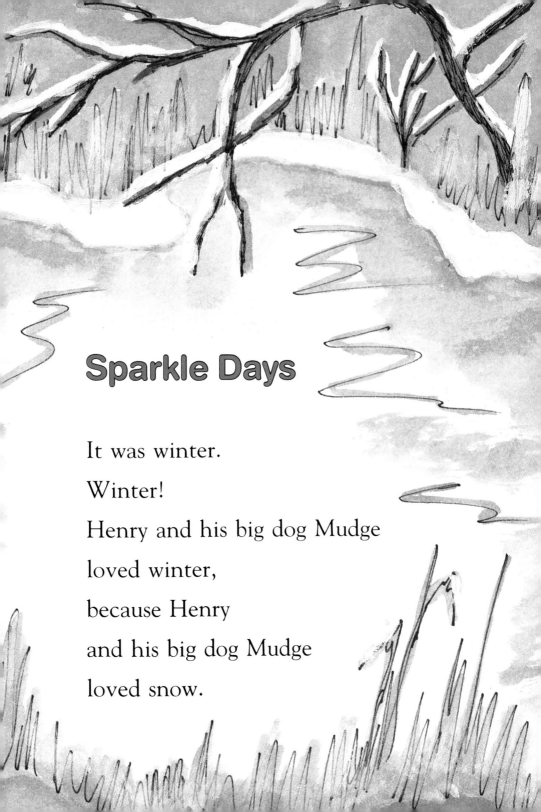

Sparkle Days

It was winter.
Winter!
Henry and his big dog Mudge
loved winter,
because Henry
and his big dog Mudge
loved snow.

This winter they were
still waiting
for the first snow.
Henry looked out his
window every morning.
"Not yet, Mudge,"
he would say.

Henry looked out his
window every night.
"Not yet, Mudge,"
he would say again.

Then one morning
Henry looked out
his window
and he shouted,
"Snow, Mudge, snow!"

He and Mudge put their noses
against the window.
They watched the snow sparkle.
They were ready for
a sparkle day.

When Henry got dressed
to go outside,
there wasn't much of Henry
to see.
He wore snow boots,
snow pants,
a snow jacket,
snow mittens,
and a snow scarf.
He also wore a snow mask
that let only
his eyes and mouth show.

When Mudge saw Henry
in his snow clothes,
he barked and barked
and barked
at the strange creature.

Then Henry took off his mask
and showed Mudge his face.
Mudge wagged his tail
and followed Henry outside.

The snow made
Henry and Mudge
want to run.
So, they ran
in circles
around the yard.

14

Mudge poked his big black nose
into the snow.

He used his nose
to dig a little hole.
Ah-choo! went Mudge.
Snow always made him sneeze.

16

Henry lay down
and made snow angels.
Mudge lay down
and messed them up.

So Henry threw a
snowball at him.
But Mudge just wagged his tail.
"Aw, Mudge," Henry said,
giving him a hug.

Henry built an icy hideout,
and they were snow spies.
There were many snow spies
in the neighborhood.

19

After four hours of playing,
they went back inside.
Henry's hands were wet
and his nose was drippy.
Mudge's paws were wet
and *his* nose was drippy.
Henry's mother wiped Henry's nose.
Henry's mother wiped Mudge's nose.

Then she put a blanket
on the floor,
and Henry and Mudge
curled up on it
and fell asleep.
Oh, did they love
sparkle days.

Christmas Eve Dinner

Every Christmas
Henry's house sparkled.
It sparkled silver.
It sparkled gold.
It had a Christmas tree
that sparkled
millions of colors.

The day before Christmas,
Henry's mother and father
always cooked a lot.
They cooked all day,
and the house smelled wonderful.

Henry's mother liked
to bake the cookies.
Henry helped her cut them
and decorate them.
She gave a lot of them away.

Henry's father liked
to bake the turkey.
He took a long time
"dressing" it.

Henry thought this was
a very funny idea.
He told Mudge,
"Dad's dressing the turkey."
Then he giggled and giggled.

In the evening
it was time
for Christmas Eve dinner.
This dinner was always fancy.
They always ate in the dining room
instead of the kitchen.

And they liked to dress up.

Even Henry.

It was the only time

he liked fancy things.

Henry's father put
a bright red cloth
on the table.
He put shiny white dishes
on top of the cloth.
Henry's mother
brought out two green
candlesticks.
She put them in the
center of the table.

Then Henry's father
carried in all the food.
Henry, his mother,
and his father
sat down to eat.
They looked at each other.
They looked at all the food.
"Wow!" Henry said.

His mother lit the candles,
and they began eating.
But while they ate,
they could hear Mudge crying.
He hadn't been invited
to the fancy Christmas Eve dinner
because he was a dog.
He had to stay in Henry's room.

Poor Mudge, thought Henry.

Poor Mudge, thought Henry's parents.

They all looked at each other.

Then Henry's father smiled.

He got up to find

an extra plate.

Henry and his mother
and his father
filled the plate with food.

Then Henry let Mudge
out of his room.
When Mudge came to the table,
Henry's father put the
plate of food
on the floor.

Henry's mother held
one of the candles
beside the plate.
Mudge wagged his tail
and began eating
as fast as he could.
It was his first fancy dinner
in the dining room.

It was his first fancy dinner
by candlelight.
"Merry Christmas, Mudge!"
said Henry.

Mudge looked at Henry
and sneezed some
fancy turkey on him.
And they laughed about that
all night long.

Firelight

On winter nights
Henry and Henry's parents
and Mudge
loved to take walks.
They loved to see
the warm lights
in the houses.

They loved to see
the winter stars
in the sky.
They loved to see
the sparkle of the moon
on the white yards.

They felt happy
on these walks.
Mudge never stopped wagging.
One night they even saw
a shooting star.
"Make a wish,"
said Henry's mother.

Henry's father wished
for peace on earth.
Henry's mother wished
for her favorite
basketball team to win.
Henry wished
for chocolate pudding
every day
for the rest of his life.
They all wondered
what Mudge wished for.
"Probably for half
of my chocolate pudding,"
said Henry.

After their walk,
they loved coming home
to their fireplace.
Henry's father and mother
sat on the couch, hugging.
Henry and Mudge
lay on the floor.

The wood popped and cracked.
No one talked much.
They just watched the flames
and thought about
sparkle days.

The house was quiet,
the room was dark,
the fire was red,
and everything
was warm.

On a winter night,
Henry
and Henry's father
and Henry's mother
and Henry's big dog Mudge
rested.